DreamWorks

DRAGONS

How to Build a DRAGON FORT

adapted by Erica David

Ready-to-Read

Simon Spotlight

New York   London   Toronto   Sydney   New Delhi

SIMON SPOTLIGHT

An imprint of Simon & Schuster Children's Publishing Division

1230 Avenue of the Americas, New York, New York 10020

This Simon Spotlight edition Febuary 2016

For information about special discounts for bulk purchases, please contact
Simon & Schuster Special Sales at 1-866-506-1949 or business@simonandschuster.com.

Manufactured in the United States of America 0116 LAK

2 4 6 8 10 9 7 5 3 1

ISBN 978-1-4814-5216-8 (hc)

ISBN 978-1-4814-5215-1 (pbk)

ISBN 978-1-4814-5217-5 (eBook)

Hiccup and his friends were on a
mission.
They wanted to find the perfect place
to build an island outpost
for themselves and their dragons—
a dragon fort.

They visited many islands,
but none felt right.
None felt like home.
And some were even dangerous!
Astrid and her dragon, Stormfly,
helped keep the Dragon Riders safe.

Finally they found a place
they liked.
Everyone was excited!
And they each had a different idea
for the fort.

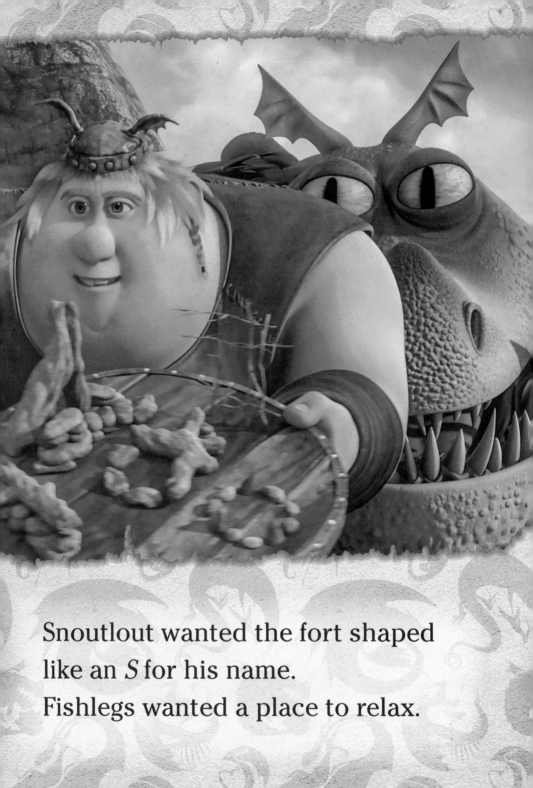

Snoutlout wanted the fort shaped
like an *S* for his name.
Fishlegs wanted a place to relax.

Astrid wanted the fort
to be well armed.
Ruffnut and Tuffnut wanted
a boar pit.

Hiccup and his dragon, Toothless,
didn't know what to do.
How could they build a fort that
would make everyone happy?

That night Tuffnut heard
a strange noise.
He went to see what it was.

In a clearing not far from the camp, Tuffnut watched as a massive dragon rose into the air.

Tuffnut ran to tell his friends.
"We have to get out of here!"
he warned them.
But they didn't believe him.
"Is anyone falling for this?"
asked Astrid.
"I'm not making this up!"
said Tuffnut.

Hiccup, Tuffnut, and Ruffnut went
to look for the giant dragon.
At first they didn't find anything.
Then they saw a dark shape up ahead.

"I don't believe it!"
said Hiccup.
The giant dragon roared and flew off.
It was headed for their camp!
Snoutlout, Fishlegs, and Astrid
were in danger!

Hiccup, Tuffnut, and Ruffnut
chased the giant dragon.
Tuffnutt and Ruffnut flew
right through it!
That's when Hiccup noticed something.

"It's not one big dragon,"
Hiccup pointed out.
"It's tons of little ones!"
The little dragons flew in a group.
Together they looked like
one big dragon!

The little dragons had a leader.
He was a small white dragon.
Tuffnut and Ruffnut captured him!

Back at the camp,
Fishlegs named the little dragons
Night Terrors.
The little white Night Terror
wasn't happy.
He wanted to get back
to the other Night Terrors.

Without their leader
the Night Terrors were in trouble!
They were under attack
from Changewings!

Hiccup and his friends flew
to the rescue!
They fought the Changewings to
protect the Night Terrors.
But they were outnumbered!

The Night Terrors needed their leader!
"They flock into the shape
of a giant version of themselves
as a defense to scare off predators,"
Fishlegs pointed out.
"Without their leader they can't!"
Hiccup said.

Hiccup zoomed back to the camp.
He released the white Night Terror.
The little dragon flew off
to join the battle.

The Changewings chased
the white Night Terror.
They were closing in when
Hiccup, Toothless, and
the other dragons
and their riders saved him!

The white Night Terror joined the rest
of his flock.
They all came together in
the shape of a huge dragon!
The Changewings were scared
of the big dragon!
They shrieked and ran away!

Hiccup and his friends cheered.

The next morning Hiccup showed
his friends a plan for the fort.
"I got the idea from the
Night Terrors," Hiccup said.
"I combined all your ideas into
one giant base!"

"We can call it the Dragon's Edge,"
said Hiccup.
"Astrid, you can make your section
heavily armed!"

"Fishlegs, your place is quiet
and relaxing," Hiccup explained.

"Snoutlout, your spot isn't S-shaped," Hiccup said. "But you can paint as many *S*'s as you like!"

"Ruffnut and Tuffnut, you can have a boar pit," Hiccup told the twins. Everyone loved Hiccup's plan.

A few days later Dragon's Edge
was complete.
"And now for one more addition,"
Hiccup announced.
The white Night Terror landed
on a perch beside Hiccup.
"The Night Terrors will be
our lookouts!" he explained.

Then the Night Terrors flocked
together.
High in the sky
they formed a dragon
shaped just like Toothless!

Toothless snorted proudly.
There was nothing like new friends
to make Dragon's Edge feel like home.